epic!

COSMIC
PIZZA PARTY

Nick Murphy • Paul Ritchey
Illustrated by
Bea Tormo

Andrews McMeel
PUBLISHING®

Cosmic Pizza Party created by Nick Murphy, Paul Ritchey, and Bea Tormo

Andrews McMeel Publishing
a division of Andrews McMeel Universal
1130 Walnut Street, Kansas City, Missouri 64106

www.andrewsmcmeel.com

Epic! Creations, Inc.
702 Marshall Street, Suite 280
Redwood City, California 94063

www.getepic.com

21 22 23 24 25 SDB 10 9 8 7 6 5 4 3 2 1

Paperback ISBN: 978-1-5248-6733-1
Hardback ISBN: 978-1-5248-6807-9

Library of Congress Control Number: 2020950784

Design by Dan Nordskog and Wendy Gable

Made by:
King Yip (Dongguan) Printing & Packaging Factory Ltd.
Address and location of manufacturer:
Daning Administrative District, Humen Town
Dongguan Guangdong, China 523930
1st Printing — 3/1/21

ATTENTION: SCHOOLS AND BUSINESSES
Andrews McMeel books are available at quantity discounts with bulk purchase for educational, business, or sales promotional use. For information, please e-mail the Andrews McMeel Publishing Special Sales Department: specialsales@amuniversal.com.

To my wife, Rebecca,
and our son, Desmond--
wanna order pizza tonight?
--Nick

Mom--thanks for all the
bedtime (and daytime) stories.
--Paul

To Fran--I love and respect you
even though you like pineapple
on your pizza.
--Bea

COSMIC
PIZZA PARTY

The Marinaris System
Life-forms come from all over the universe to sample the delectable pizza this system is known for.

PLANET PAPA
Once a quiet, peaceful planet, it is now one big Papa Roni's Restau-Roni. Current wait time for a seat is four rotations.

BRIAR IV
Meg's home planet. Thick jungles and lush greenery cover this entire planet. The Briar IV populace enjoys a slow and steady lifestyle.

CALZONIA
The queen regent rules this planet, known for its prison pits and parties.

NACI
Suzie's home planet. The sluglike inhabitants created mechanical suits to protect them from the hazardous terrain.

AVIS
The crown jewel of Avis is QUILLADELPHIA, the planet of featherly love.

SYLCON-5
A planet covered in silicone. The planet's original inhabitants left thousands of years ago. It's now home to the Plegans.

BIOS.sys
This planet contains the Cyber Forge, source of all sentient robotic life.

RODENTIA
This system's Ratonian food festival should be on everyone's calendar every solstice. Space pirates also tell tales of a planet rich with cheese.

CRYSTALIS
Mohs's home planet. The rocklike Crystali are constantly at war with the Paparions and Scizaros.

SKARABSGAARD
Its arid landscape and dangerous winds create massive dust- and sandstorms. Its insect inhabitants use stormcrawlers to navigate the storms.

CHAPTER 1
Nothing to Cheese At

IT'S HERE!

THE PAPA RONI'S FAST-RISING DOUGH I ORDERED FROM ASTRONOMY PRIME!

UGH, BOXED DOUGH?

HOW MUCH WAS THAT? DID YOU USE THE COMPANY CARD?

WE'RE ON A TIGHT BUDGET...

BUT IT'S FAST-RISING! WE CAN MAKE MORE PIZZAS FASTER AND MAKE MORE CREDITS...FASTER.

PLUS, THEY DELIVERED IT IN LESS THAN TWO PARSECS!

Wow, the dough Suzie makes never glows...

3

4

PAPA RONI'S PIZZA RESTAU-RONI. THE GALAXY'S MOST FAMOUS RESTAU-RONI. DECENT INGREDIENTS. DECENT PIZZA.

REMINDS ME OF THE EARLY DAYS...

...FUMBLING MY WAY. TRYING TO GET AS MANY PIZZAS INTO AS MANY BELLIES AS POSSIBLE.

HUGE FAN, MR. RONI. I'VE WATCHED ALL YOUR VLOOOOOG--

WHOMP!

I'M FAR TOO BUSY TO BE THERE IN PERSON. HOLOGRAM TECHNOLOGY IS THE ONLY WAY TO DO BUSINESS THESE DAYS.

I LIKE TO KEEP TABS ON THE LITTLE GUYS. YOU'RE TOUGH TO TRACK.

MOBILE PIZZA TRUCK, HUH? SEEMS LIKE A LOT OF RUNNING AROUND.

WE BRING THE PIZZA TO THE PEOPLE. FAST.

THE BEST PIZZA.

BEST TRY!

AT A FAIR PRICE.

GET ONE PIZZA -MAYBE PAY LATER?

THIS PLANET...

WELL.

SOME DO SAY GREAT DANGER SLUMBERS AMONG THE CURDS.

BUT THAT'S PROBABLY ALL JUST TALK.

AND IF YOU COULD MAKE A PIZZA WITH THIS CHEESE, YOU'D HAVE THE SECOND-TASTIEST PIZZA IN THE GALAXY.

YOU'D BE DELIVERING FROM HERE TO THE EDGE OF THE UNIVERSE.

AND, MOST IMPORTANTLY, YOU'D BE *RICH!*

NO MORE COUPONS?

NO MORE COUPONS.

SO WHY DON'T YOU GO GET IT?

BECAUSE IT'S RISKY. AND RISK IS BAD FOR BIG BUSINESS.

WELP! GOTTA JET. CATCH YA LATER.

AL-N, IF WE CAN FIND THIS CHEESE, MAYBE SUZIE WILL FINALLY HAVE THE RIGHT INGREDIENTS TO MAKE THE PERFECT PIZZA.

And if the pizza is good, Mohs will surely be happy with the excess profits.

YOU KNOW WHAT MOHS ALWAYS SAYS ABOUT PROFITS...

WHOOP-WHOOP WHOOP

NO, HE ALWAYS SAYS *CHA-CHING!*

That was actually my scanner alarm going off. Dairy detected.

Papa Roni was correct.

It is quite primo.

PIE-IN-THE-SKY, WE ARE GO FOR CHEESE RETRIEVAL.

SLICE 1, WAIT! WE HIT SOME HYPER-SPACE TRAFFIC.

NO CAN DO. THAR BE CHEESE!

UH, GUYS, REMEMBER WHEN PAPA RONI SAID THAT GREAT DANGER SLUMBERED AMONG THE CURDS?

WELL, WE KIND OF WOKE IT UP!

THAT'S PAPA RONI'S SHIP!

THAT DOUBLE-CROSSER IS STEALING ALL THE CHEESE WHILE WE GET EATEN!

The worm is very close to consuming us.

I would prefer that we are not consumed.

DON'T WORRY. I'LL LOSE HIM WITH SOME SICK MANEUVERS.

Was your plan to have the worm smash those rocks?

NO, THAT WAS NOT THE PLAN, AL-N!

PAPA TROOPERS-- KEEP A LOOKOUT FOR THOSE GULLIBLE FOOLS!

ANYONE IMPULSIVE ENOUGH TO BUY MY FAST-RISE DOUGH WAS SURE TO BELIEVE MY CHEESE "TIP."

THEY WERE THE PERFECT WORM BAIT!

23

CHAPTER 2
Pizza Power-Up

SCORE
421307

LIFE

START

27

IS IT A NEW OVEN?

IT'S BETTER THAN THAT.

AN OVEN THAT CAN CRANK OUT PIZZAS FASTER THAN I CAN DELIVER THEM?

THINK BIGGER!

IT'S WAY COOLER THAN THAT.

IT'S A QUANTUM REALITY MACHINE!

A QUAN- WHAT NOW?

A QR MACHINE IS THE MOST CUTTING-EDGE VIDEO GAME SYSTEM IN THE GALAXY.

I GOT US A GIG BY ADVERTISING THAT WE HAVE VIDEO GAMES *AND* PIZZA!

BE THE FIRST TO PLAY THE GALAXY'S MOST EXTREME VIDEO GAME!!!

ALSO, WE HAVE PIZZA

Calzonia Palace, Marinaris System.

Prince Antonio Calzonio's eleventh sun-turning party.

HAPPY BIRTHDAY

Mohs's QR machine was quite popular at the party.

Especially with Prince Antonio, who played nonstop for 2.7 hours.

WHOA! THIS THING IS *WIZARD!*

Perhaps it is customary in Calzonia for party guests to wait to eat until their prince has finished his game.

IS IT CUSTOMARY TO LET YOUR PIZZA GET COLD?

BARBARIANS...

MAYBE WE JUST HAVE TO SHOVE IT IN THEIR FACES.

SPLAT!

FZZTT!

MY SON!

WHAT HAVE YOU DONE WITH HIM?!

Suzie, it appears our delicious pizza has caused a power malfunction in the QR machine.

The Prince seems to have been teleported into the video game dimension.

GET MY SON BACK THIS INSTANT!

OR IT'S OFF TO THE PRISON PITS WITH ALL OF YOU!

OH NO! PRISON WILL BE TERRIBLE FOR OUR PROFITS.

NO WORRIES.

I CAN FIX THIS. WE'LL GET THE PRINCE OUT LICKETY-SPLIT.

WAIT, MEG!

34

36

RESCUE MY SON!

HI, MOM!

UHHH...WHY IS THE QUEEN ON A GIANT SCREEN IN THE SKY?

She is watching us "play" the game from outside of this reality.

THIS VIDEO GAME IS DANGEROUS!

IT FEELS SO REAL.

IT'S NOT A VIDEO GAME, IT'S A VIDEO GAME PLUS REAL LIFE.

SO IF IT'S NOT JUST A GAME ANYMORE...

IT WORKED, MOHS!

THIS IS JUST LIKE TOSSING A PIZZA.

THAT'S WHAT I DO BEST!

YOU WHIPPED THAT DOUGH INTO A FRENZY!

THINK YOU CAN WHIP MEG BACK INTO THE ACTION?

ACHIEVEMENT UNLOCKED: DARING RESCUE COMPLETE!

YOU SAVED MY BOY!

WE'RE NOT OUT OF THIS YET, GUYS.

WE'VE STILL GOT TROUBLE.

GRRRR!

47

48

The Queen was overjoyed to have her son returned to her in one piece.

As an apology, we gifted the QR machine to Prince Antonio...

...after we made a couple of safety tweaks, of course.

Mohs was sad to give away his QR machine, but Suzie and Meg reminded him that video games are not the team's specialty. He apologized and promised to talk to the crew before buying any new equipment.

Plus, he felt a lot better once we got back to what we are really best at--making pizzas.

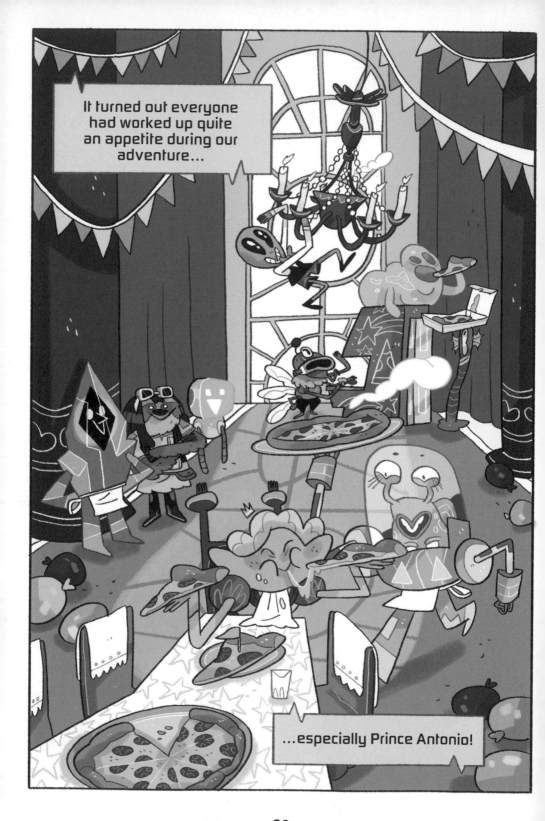

It turned out everyone had worked up quite an appetite during our adventure...

...especially Prince Antonio!

CHAPTER 3
Scrap Iron Chef

THIS SHOULD BE THE SCORE THAT MOVES US PAST PAPA RONI...

A BAD REVIEW?!

I CAN'T BELIEVE THIS!

△ CHEWber Eats ▽

👍 PAPA RONI
3.9.

👎 THE COSMIC PIZZA PARTY
3.8.

SUZIE, WE HAVE BIGGER PROBLEMS.

I CAN BARELY MAKE MY DELIVERIES. I AM LITERALLY DROWNING IN TRASH.

Yes, the influx of new customers has left little time for maintenance and cleaning.

SUZIE, WHEN YOU ADVERTISE FROM HERE TO TIMBUK-4, YOU'RE GONNA GET A FEW BAD REVIEWS.

BRUTALFOODDOOD25 SAYS OUR PIZZA IS INEDIBLE!

The poor review is from Sylcon-5.

It is a planet populated by plastic-eating people called Plegans.

55

DID YOU MEAN BRUTALFOODDOOD...25?

YEAH! THAT ONE!

HERE!!!

IS THAT "PIZZA"? WE'VE TRIED! IT'S INEDIBLE!

PLEGANS CAN'T DIGEST THE ORGANIC MATERIALS.

WE'RE REALLY SORRY ABOUT OUR FRIEND'S TEMPER.

SHE GOT PRETTY WORKED UP OVER YOUR REVIEW.

MY REVIEW?

PEOPLE ACTUALLY *READ* THOSE?

THEY RUIN LIVES!

LATER...

Suzie, you understand now that the Plegans cannot eat your food. It is not your fault.

MY GOAL IS TO MAKE EVERY PERSON, IN EVERY PART OF THE GALAXY, HAPPY WITH MY FOOD.

IT'S THE GASTRONOMIC OATH: "ALL FOR FOOD, AND FOOD FOR ALL."

As a synthetic being, I am sympathetic to the Plegans' complaints. But I also understand Suzie's desire to please them.

WELL, MAYBE WE FOCUS ON A PROBLEM WE CAN SOLVE?

LIKE CLEANING UP OUR SHIP.

RIGHT, SUZIE?

SUZIE!?

I NEED TO CLEAR MY HEAD.

GREAT. HOW ARE WE GOING TO KEEP UP WITH ORDERS NOW THAT OUR STAR CHEF IS GONE?

HELLO?

I DIDN'T REALIZE MY REVIEW WOULD CAUSE SO MANY PROBLEMS.

SUZIE TAKES HER COOKING VERY SERIOUSLY.

SOMETIMES A LITTLE **TOO** SERIOUSLY. WE JUST NEED TO LET HER COOL OFF.

IF YOUR PEOPLE CAN'T EAT ORGANIC FOOD...

...WHY EVEN ORDER IT?

WELL, TO BE HONEST, WE'VE GOTTEN A LITTLE DESPERATE.

LET ME TRY TO EXPLAIN...

64

THAT'S TRUE... ...BUT AT LEAST I COULD EAT THE REST OF THE INGREDIENTS.

PLEGAN FOOD IS TOTALLY *DIFFERENT.*

YOU'RE RIGHT. IT'S A BIGGER CHALLENGE.

AND TO GROW AS A CHEF, YOU MUST CONFRONT DIFFERENT AND LARGER CHALLENGES.

YOU SHOULD NEVER BE AFRAID TO ASK FOR HELP.

ASK OTHERS FOR ADVICE AND CRITIQUES. THAT'S HOW THEY CAN HELP YOU IMPROVE.

YOU KNOW WHAT? YOU'RE RIGHT, CHEF.

MMMM...

I NEED YOUR HELP.

OKAY.

LET'S BEGIN.

MEANWHILE...

I am detecting silicates and organic materials in these caverns.

WELL, ONLY ONE WAY TO FIND OUT WHAT'S IN THERE.

LET'S GO INSIDE.

WOW, THIS PLACE MAKES EVEN *OUR* SHIP LOOK CLEAN.

It appears the Plegan miners abandoned their efforts once they became sick from the high levels of organic materials.

My scanners indicate silicates directly below.

But there's a strong organic component, as well...

LET'S DIG IN!!!

BACK AT CHEF JULIENNE'S HOME...

THIS LOOKS DELICIOUS!

YOU LIKE IT?

OH YES!

I WISH YOU COULD TASTE IT, BUT IT WOULDN'T BE SAFE FOR YOU TO EAT.

I HAVE TO GO TELL MY FRIENDS.

WITH ALL THE TRASH FROM OUR SHIP, WE CAN HELP WITH YOUR PLANET'S FOOD SHORTAGE!

REMEMBER: TRUST YOUR RECIPES...

...IT'S OKAY TO ASK FOR HELP...

SHOOOM!!!

...AND THINK OUTSIDE THE PIZZA BOX!

KNOCK KNOCK!

YOUR FRIENDS?

THEY'VE BEEN GONE FOR HOURS. I'M A LITTLE WORRIED.

I'LL PUT THEIR LAST KNOWN LOCATION IN YOUR GPS.

I'VE GOT TO FIND THEM.

COME ON, SLICE 1! GO!

FSSHH-OOM!!

THIS MUST BE THE PLACE...

OH NO.

I HOPE I'M NOT TOO LATE.

PLEASE BE OKAY! PLEASE BE OKAY! PLEASE BE OKAY!

CHAPTER 4
Delivery Dilemma

UNBELIEVABLE!

HOW'D THE DELIVERY GO?

COOK ME UP ANOTHER PIE.

I'M HEADING BACK DOWN.

NO WAY--IT DIDN'T MAKE IT?

The storms have increased in intensity faster than I predicted.

It would be dangerous to attempt another delivery now.

I ALREADY PROMISED HIM ANOTHER ONE, SO FIRE UP THE OVEN.

ANOTHER ONE?!

IF HIS DRONES CAN MAKE THESE DELIVERIES...

...THEN THERE HAS TO BE A WAY FOR ME TO DO IT IN SLICE 1.

PAPA'S PIZZAS ARE MADE SO CHEAP, HE CAN AFFORD A WHOLE ARMY OF DELIVERY DRONES.

HE'S CHARGING TWICE THE PRICE FOR PIZZA THAT'S HALF AS GOOD!

ALL BECAUSE HIS DRONES ARE THE ONLY THINGS THAT CAN GET THROUGH THOSE STORMS.

I'M GOING TO FOLLOW THEM.

MAYBE I CAN FIGURE OUT A TRICK TO NAVIGATE THE STORM.

KEEP AN EYE ON HER, AL-N.

DON'T LET HER GET *TOO* ADVENTUROUS.

Meg made upgrades to the Slice 1 all through the night.

She took boxes of cooking utensils that Suzie was not using.

Well, Suzie was *going* to use them, but had not opened them yet.

A heavy-duty hand mixer + industrial-grade fork = a new tow cable...

Heat-resistant steel roasting pans = emergency sled legs...

And a supersecret ingredient that Meg refused to tell anyone about.

THANKS FOR THE LIFT!

NO PROBLEM!

THINK I CAN GET THAT PIZZA NOW?

BACK ABOARD THE PIE-IN-THE-SKY...

I'M SORRY, EVERYONE.

I REALLY MESSED THINGS UP.

MY STUPID PRIDE LOST US A BUNCH OF MONEY *AND* SLICE 1.

IT'S ONLY A SHIP, MEG.

WE'RE JUST HAPPY YOU'RE OKAY.

LOOK, LOSING SLICE 1 IS AN EXPENSIVE LESSON.

BUT WE'RE A TEAM! WE FIGURE THINGS OUT!

PLUS, I'VE BEEN TELLING MOHS TO SELL THAT OLD HUNK OF JUNK AND BUY YOU A NEW SHIP FOR MONTHS.

CHAPTER 5
REALITY SHOWDOWN

THE WINNER OF THIS COMPETITION WILL BE AWARDED A PIECE OF...

...THE *EVER DOUGH!*

THIS FAMED STARTER DOUGH COMES FROM UNKNOWN REACHES OF THE COSMOS. IT'S BEEN HANDED DOWN FROM CHEF TO CHEF FOR MILLENNIA.

NO ONE CAN EXPLAIN ITS MYSTICAL POWER TO REGENERATE ITSELF.

NOW!

LET'S PLAY SOME GAMES!

BUT FIRST, PAPA...

...IT APPEARS YOUR TEAM DOES NOT HAVE THE REQUIRED FOUR CONTESTANTS.

OH, WE HAVE A FOURTH.

SEND IN...

...SUPREME!

CRASH!

MEET THE LATEST IN ANDROID-MASCOT TECHNOLOGY.

I'VE PROGRAMMED SUPREME TO EXCEL AT EVERY TASK.

WHOA! THEY HAVE THEIR OWN AL-N?

HA!

SUPREME IS WAY BETTER THAN YOUR JUNKY OLD ROBOT.

PAPA SAYS EVERY PAPA RONI PIZZA JOINT IS GONNA HAVE A SUPREME IN IT BY THE END OF THE YEAR.

109

SWIPE!

SPLASH!

SMASH!

GULP!

DELIVERY FOR MR. SOLARI.

TEAM COSMIC PIZZA PARTY WINS!

ANOTHER EXCITING END TO *THE SLICE IS RIGHT.*

127

ABOUT THE AUTHORS

NICK MURPHY IS A FILMMAKER AND CO-HOSTS THE PODCAST *PRETEND FRIENDS*. HE'S A GRADUATE OF THE UNIVERSITY OF THE ARTS. NICK ENJOYS REPETITION, POP CULTURE, THE '80s, TIME TRAVEL, STAR WARS, REPETITION, TUNNELS, 24 FPS, REPETITION, BEING COLOR-BLIND, AND WRITING HIS BIOGRAPHY. HE CURRENTLY LIVES IN PHILADELPHIA WITH HIS WIFE, ARTIST REBECCA CHEWNING, AND THEIR AWESOME SON, DESMOND.

PAUL RITCHEY IS A FILMMAKER AND WEB HOST LIVING IN PHILADELPHIA. HE HOSTS *CONTINUE?*, A WEEKLY GAMING COMEDY SHOW. HE ALSO PERFORMS ON *PRETEND FRIENDS*, AN ACTUAL-PLAY TABLETOP ROLE-PLAYING SHOW. PAUL IS SO FAST THAT HIS MOVEMENTS ARE BEYOND HUMAN RECOGNITION. SOME QUESTION HIS QUICKNESS, BUT THAT IS ONLY BECAUSE HIS SPEED IS SO BEYOND HUMAN RECOGNITION THAT HE APPEARS TO BE STANDING STILL.

ABOUT THE ILLUSTRATOR

BEA TORMO IS A CHILDREN'S BOOK ILLUSTRATOR BY DAY AND A COMIC BOOK ARTIST BY NIGHT. SHE LIVES NEAR BARCELONA, SPAIN, WHERE SHE ENJOYS BEING PART OF A COMMUNITY OF ARTISTS. BESIDES CHILDREN'S BOOKS AND COMICS, BEA WORKS ON MAGAZINES, WEBCOMICS, AND FANZINES. SHE ESPECIALLY LOVES DRAWING GRUMPY PEOPLE AND MONSTERS.

MEET THE
COSMIC PIZZA PARTY TEAM!

MEG

ACE DELIVERY DRIVER. THE INTERGALACTIC SLOTH
MAY LOOK SLOW, BUT WHEN SHE'S PILOTING HER
DELIVERY SHIP--THE SLICE 1--SHE'S FASTER
THAN A SLICE OF PIZZA BEING GOBBLED UP AT A
BIRTHDAY PARTY. BOLD AND READY FOR AN
ADVENTURE, MEG ZOOMS HEADFIRST INTO
EACH DELIVERY WITH HER BEST BUD, AL-N.

AL-N

ROBOTIC INTERN. THIS ANDROID IS TRYING TO
LEARN ALL HE CAN ABOUT THE PIZZA BUSINESS
WHILE METICULOUSLY LOGGING ALL OF THE CREW'S
ADVENTURES. THE INTERNSHIP POSTING READ,
"TRAVEL THE GALAXY, VISIT EXCITING LOCALES, MEET
INTERESTING CLIENTELE, AND EAT ALL THE PIZZA YOU
WANT!" IT WAS A DREAM COME TRUE...EXCEPT FOR
THAT LAST PART. AL-N DISCOVERED THAT EATING
PIZZA DOESN'T AGREE WITH HIS CIRCUITRY.

SUZIE

HEAD CHEF AND CHIEF PIZZA OFFICER. THIS MECHA-SLUG IS A TRUE PIZZA GENIUS. SUZIE IS DEVOTED TO THE GASTRONOMIC OATH: "ALL FOR FOOD, AND FOOD FOR ALL!" THAT MEANS SHE SPENDS EVERY MOMENT OF HER DAY THINKING UP NEW WAYS TO MAKE HER PIZZAS EVEN MORE DELICIOUS. SUZIE HAS A BIT OF A TEMPER, THOUGH, SO IF YOU WANT TO GIVE HER SOME PIZZA FEEDBACK, DO IT FAST AND PREPARE TO DUCK FOR COVER!

COSMIC
PIZZA TRUCK

From outrunning space worms
to delivering the best pizza
in the galaxy, the pizza truck is
essential to the Cosmic Pizza team.

RIGHT ENGINE
ALSO GRATES
CHEESE

LOUNGE
MOHS'S FAVORITE
PLACE TO CRUNCH
THE CREDITS

COCKPIT
MEG'S DOMAIN

**AL-N'S
CHARGING
STATION**
WITH NO-SCUFF
SCREEN-
POLISHING
PILLOW

ROOF LADDER
WINDOW IS SECURED BY "PLASMA-SEAL INSTANT COAGULATING" TECH

CLOSET
WHERE MEG IS *SUPPOSED* TO STORE HER TOOLS

SLEEPING QUARTERS
WHO HAS TIME TO SLEEP? WE'VE GOT PIZZAS TO DELIVER

PANTRY
FULL OF ONLY THE BEST, 100% ALL-NATURAL INGREDIENTS

KITCHEN
UNLESS YOU'RE SUZIE, KEEP OUT!

ENTROPY-FREE STAR-FIRED OVEN
PERFECTLY CRISP CRUST, EVERY TIME

WHO IS YOUR PERFECT PIZZA PAL?

Answer a few questions about pizza, and we'll let you know who your pizzeria BFF is!

1. WHAT IS YOUR FAVORITE TOPPING?
   A. ALL OF THEM! I LOVE PIZZA SO MUCH THAT I WANT IT ALL!
   B. PEPPERONI AND CHEESE. IT'S A CLASSIC FOR A REASON!
   C. TOPPINGS? THOSE ARE EXPENSIVE. LET'S NOT GO OVERBOARD HERE.

2. HOW MANY SLICES DO YOU EAT?
   A. SLICES? I EAT A WHOLE PIZZA IN A SINGLE BITE.
   B. JUST ENOUGH. I WANT TO SAMPLE AND SAVOR EVERY BITE, BUT I DON'T WANT TO GET SICK.
   C. JUST ONE SLICE A DAY. A WHOLE PIZZA CAN LAST ME A WEEK!

3. HOW DO YOU EAT YOUR PIZZA?
   A. DON'T TELL ANYONE, BUT SOMETIMES I BITE THE CRUST FIRST.
   B. ONE SLICE AT A TIME. I DIDN'T KNOW THIS WAS UP FOR DEBATE.
   C. WITH A FORK AND KNIFE, LIKE A CIVILIZED PERSON (OR ALIEN)!

4. WHAT'S YOUR PIZZA DELIVERY MOTTO?
   A. ALWAYS HOT. ALWAYS ON TIME. ALWAYS DELICIOUS.
   B. THE PERFECT PIZZA, OR YOU'RE WRONG.
   C. THE FIRST TOPPING IS FREE! (DOUGH COUNTS AS A TOPPING, RIGHT?)

5. WHAT KIND OF CRUST?
   A. THE THICKER THE BETTER. MORE PIZZA = YUM.
   B. NOT TOO THICK, NOT TOO THIN. A GOOD PIZZA IS ALL ABOUT BALANCE.
   C. PAPER THIN, SO WE CAN MAKE MORE PIZZAS WITH LESS DOUGH.

6. WHICH PLANET WOULD YOU MAKE A DELIVERY TO FIRST?
   A. FIRST?! I'D GO TO EVERY PLANET AS QUICKLY AS POSSIBLE.
   B. THE PLANET WITH THE RICHEST CULINARY SCENE.
   C. WHICHEVER ONE HAS THE MOST MONEY.

7. DO YOU LIKE COLD PIZZA?
   A. COLD? I'VE NEVER LET A PIZZA GO COLD IN MY LIFE!
   B. ARE YOU SERIOUS? PIZZA NEEDS TO BE ENJOYED FRESH OUT OF THE OVEN.
   C. OF COURSE! I NEVER LET ANY PIZZA (OR MONEY) GO TO WASTE.

8. **WHAT IS YOUR LEAST FAVORITE PIZZA?**
   A. RED GIANT TOMATO PIE
   B. PLUTONIUM PINEAPPLE PIZZA! YUCK!
   C. BETELGEUSE DEEP DISH

9. **WHEN IS THE BEST TIME TO EAT PIZZA?**
   A. ANYTIME! BREAKFAST, LUNCH, DOUBLE LUNCH, PRE-DINNER, AND EVEN DESSERT!
   B. WHEN IT'S RIGHT OUT OF THE OVEN AT A SAFE BUT OPTIMAL TEMPERATURE.
   C. WHEN SOMEONE ELSE IS PAYING!

10. **AND FOR THE FINAL QUESTION, SPONSORED BY PAPA RONI PIZZA RESTAU-RONI™, WHO MAKES THE BEST PIZZA IN THE GALAXY?**
    A. ~~PAPA RONI~~ COSMIC PIZZA PARTY
    B. ~~PAPA RONI~~ COSMIC PIZZA PARTY
    C. ~~PAPA RONI~~ COSMIC PIZZA PARTY

IF YOU MOSTLY ANSWERED A:

Your best pal is Meg! You both just love pizza--it's as simple as that. You'll eat pizza any way it's made, but you also know exactly what you love the most. You're always ready to leap face-first into the next pizza adventure. There's plenty of pizza excitement in your future!

IF YOU MOSTLY ANSWERED B:

Suzie is your pizza bud. You're a pizza purist! You appreciate the fine art of "Pizzaioli." You bow at the altar of the supreme pizza trinity: dough, sauce, and cheese. People will call you a foodie, and that's fine, because way down in your deep dish of hearts, you know what you are: a connoisseur.

IF YOU MOSTLY ANSWERED C:

You and Mohs are kindred pizza spirits. Pizza is your business. Literally. You spend all day finding the most cost-efficient way to make the most pizzas--and then finding the customers who will buy them from you! Truth be told, you'd probably rather have money than pizza, but that one time you tried to bite a Space Credit, you almost cracked a tooth.

PAPA RONI'S BUSINESS QUIZ

Hello, I am AL-N. After my internship with the Cosmic Pizza Party crew, I decided to take Papa Roni's Guide to Pizza Business Success course. Help me answer these questions to see if we both learned the best way to run a pizza company.

1. FIND THE CHEAPEST INGREDIENTS POSSIBLE. NEVER WORRY ABOUT QUALITY.
   TRUE OR FALSE

2. NEVER PAY FULL PRICE BECAUSE THEY'RE PROBABLY RIPPING YOU OFF.
   TRUE OR FALSE

3. IF A CUSTOMER SAYS THAT YOU MADE A MISTAKE, JUST CHARGE THEM TWICE AS MUCH TO FIX IT.
   TRUE OR FALSE

4. THERE'S NOTHING WRONG WITH STEALING IDEAS, ESPECIALLY IF THEY'RE BETTER THAN YOURS.
   TRUE OR FALSE

5. IT'S TOTALLY FINE TO USE SOMEONE ELSE'S BETTER-LOOKING PIZZA IN YOUR ADVERTISEMENTS.
   TRUE OR FALSE

6. MASCOTS SHOULD BE BIG, SCARY, AND INTIMIDATING.
   TRUE OR FALSE

7. NEVER GIVE YOUR EMPLOYEES A RAISE.
   TRUE OR FALSE

8. IF A CUSTOMER HAS A COUPON, TELL THEM YOU DON'T ACCEPT COUPONS--EVEN IF YOU GAVE IT TO THEM THE WEEK BEFORE!
   TRUE OR FALSE

9. BUSINESS PLANS ARE FOR SUCKERS.
   TRUE OR FALSE

10. LYING IS OKAY AS LONG AS YOU GET PAID.
    TRUE OR FALSE

11. IF SOMEONE SAYS YOU'RE BREAKING THE LAW,
    TELL 'EM TO TAKE YOU TO COURT AND PROVE IT.
    TRUE OR FALSE

12. IF A CUSTOMER SAYS THAT THEY CAN GET BETTER PIZZA
    SOMEWHERE ELSE, BAN THEM FOR LIFE.
    TRUE OR FALSE

IF YOU HAD MORE TRUE ANSWERS:

You passed Papa Roni's course... but that might not be a good thing. Papa can be pretty careless toward others when it comes to his business practices. Being successful is good, but being kind and caring to your customers and friends is important, too!

IF YOU HAD MORE FALSE ANSWERS:

That's the ticket! Running a business requires a lot of hard choices. Making money is important, but being respectful and thoughtful to your customers is important, too. You're on your way to making sure your business is out of this (and every) world!

PIE-IN-THE-SKY PIZZA

Suzie learned in *Cosmic Pizza Party: Scrap Iron Chef* that not everyone enjoys the same foods. This recipe lets you explore the flavors you like best. Don't forget to ask for help if you need it. All for food, and food for all!

FOR THE DOUGH (MAKES TWO 12-INCH PIES):
2 to 3 cups all-purpose flour
1 package (2 1/4 teaspoons) active dry yeast
1 teaspoon sugar
1/2 teaspoon salt
1 cup warm water (approximately 110°F)
2 tablespoons olive oil
Cooking spray

TOPPINGS FOR TRADITIONAL CHEESE PIZZA (double for two pies):
1/2 cup tomato or pizza sauce
1 cup pizza cheese, shredded
(a blend of mozzarella, provolone, and parmesan cheeses)

1. In a large bowl, combine 2 cups of the flour with the yeast, sugar, and salt.

2. Add the water and oil and mix with a spoon or your hands until the dough comes together to form a ball. If the dough is too sticky, add flour 1 tablespoon at a time. If the dough is too dry or crumbly, add water 1 tablespoon at a time.

3. Turn the dough onto a lightly floured surface and knead by pushing the dough into the surface and away from you, then folding it in half and repeating the process.

4. Knead the dough for 8 to 10 minutes, or until you can form it into a smooth, firm ball.

5. Lightly coat a clean bowl with cooking spray. Place the ball of dough in the bowl and cover it with plastic wrap. Place the bowl in a warm spot and let the dough rise for 20 minutes. It should double in size. Ask a grown-up to preheat the oven to 450°F.

6. Remove the dough from the bowl, divide it into two equal pieces, and then stretch and flatten both pieces into discs with your hands. Place the dough on a pizza pan or baking sheet and stretch it to the edges with your fingertips.

7. Spread sauce on the pizza dough, leaving 1/2 inch uncovered around the edge.

8. Sprinkle the cheese on top of the sauce.

9. Bake for 10 to 15 minutes, or until the crust is golden brown and the cheese is bubbly.

INSTEAD OF TOMATO SAUCE, TRY:

Ricotta cheese
Olive oil
Pesto
Barbecue sauce
Hummus

OUT-OF-THIS-WORLD TOPPINGS TO TRY:

Ham
Bell peppers
Eggs
Mushrooms
Arugula

Light-Speed Delivery:

Use a store-bought pizza shell, a bagel, or even a flour tortilla for the base of your pizza. Just don't tell Suzie!

SUZIE'S STELLAR FRUIT PIZZA

Pizza should be enjoyed all the time--even for dessert! Suzie created this recipe for the Applevores, an alien race that only eats fruit. Get a grown-up's help with the oven, and you'll be on your way to a delectable dessert.

FOR THE CRUST:
1/2 cup butter, softened (1 stick)
3/4 cup sugar
1 teaspoon vanilla extract
2 cups all-purpose flour
1 teaspoon baking soda
1/4 teaspoon salt
2 tablespoons milk
Cooking spray

FOR THE TOPPING:
8 ounces mascarpone or softened cream cheese
1/2 cup powdered sugar
4 ounces whipped topping
2 cups sliced soft fruit such as peaches, berries, bananas, mango, mandarin oranges, figs, or kiwifruit
2 tablespoons honey

1. Ask a grown-up to preheat the oven to 350°F. In a large mixing bowl, combine the butter, sugar, and vanilla.

2. In a separate bowl, combine the flour, baking soda, and salt. Add the dry ingredients to the butter mixture, and use your hands to combine until you have fine crumbs.

3. Add the milk and knead to combine. If the mixture is too dry, gradually add milk until you can form a ball with the dough.

4. Lightly coat a baking sheet or pizza pan with cooking spray. Use floured hands or a rolling pin to spread the dough evenly, about 1/4 inch thick. Poke holes in the crust with a fork.

5. Ask a grown-up to help you bake the crust for 12 to 15 minutes, or until light golden brown. Remove from the oven and let cool completely. In a clean bowl, mix the cheese and sugar well, and fold in the whipped topping.

6. Spread the cheese mixture on the crust, leaving 1/2 inch uncovered around the edge.

7. Top with the fruit, drizzle with the honey, and enjoy!

How would YOU draw the Cosmic Pizza Party crew? These amazing artists show us their takes!

Pin-Ups

Suzie's Pie-in-the-Sky:
David Vordtriede

Meg's Mini Pizza Party:
Aliza Layne

Eat at Papa's!:
Ryan Goldsberry

Pizza Surfing:
Joey Ellis

EXTRA BEES ☐ DRY ☐ SMELL ☐ WH
☐ MYSTERIOUS SAUCE ☐ LEAVES ☐ HU

HAVE YOU HEARD ABOUT epic! YET?

We're the largest digital library for kids, used by millions in homes and schools around the world. We love stories so much that we're now creating our own!

With the help of some of the best writers and illustrators in the world, we create the wildest adventures we can think of. Like a mermaid and a narwhal who solve mysteries. Or a pet made out of slime.

We hope you have as much fun reading our books as we had making them!

LOOK FOR THESE BOOKS FROM

epic!

AVAILABLE **NOW!**

TO READ MORE, VISIT
getepic.com